D1047180

DATE DUE

GAYLORD			PRINTED IN U.S.A.

Three Blind Mice

The Whole Story

John W. Ivimey

Illustrated by Walton Corbould

Derrydale Books

New York · Avenel

This 1995 edition is published by Derrydale Books,
distributed by Random House Value Publishing, Inc.
40 Engelhard Avenue
Avenel, New Jersey 07001

Random House
New York · Toronto · London · Sydney · Auckland

Printed and bound in Singapore

Library of Congress Cataloging-in-Publication Data

8 7 6 5 4 3 2 1

Three Blind Mice

Round for Three Voices

Twice through and finish at pause.

Three Small Mice,
Three Small Mice,

Pined for some fun,
Pined for some fun.

They made up their minds to set out to roam;
Said they, "'Tis dull to remain at home,"
And all the luggage they took was a comb,

These three Small Mice.

Three Bold Mice,
Three Bold Mice,

Came to an inn,
Came to an inn.

"Good evening, Host, can you give us a bed?"
But the host he grinned and he shook his head,
So they all slept out in a field instead,

    These three Bold Mice.

Three Cold Mice,
Three Cold Mice,

Woke up next morn,
Woke up next morn.

They each had a cold and a swollen face,
Through sleeping all night in an open space,
So they rose quite early and left the place,

These three Cold Mice.

Three Hungry Mice,
Three Hungry Mice,

Searched for some food,
Searched for some food.

But all they found was a walnut shell
That lay by the side of a dried-up well.
Who had eaten the nut they could not tell,

These three Hungry Mice.

Three Starved Mice,
Three Starved Mice,

Came to a farm,
Came to a farm.

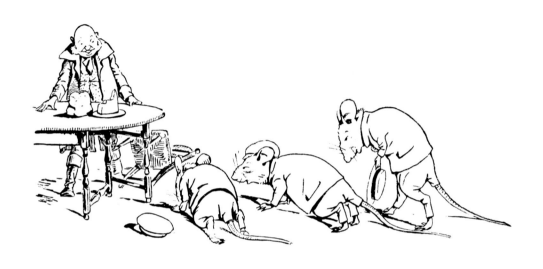

The farmer was eating some bread and cheese;
So they all went down on their hands and knees,
And squeaked, "Pray, give us a morsel, please,"

These three Starved Mice.

Three Glad Mice,
Three Glad Mice,

Ate all they could,
Ate all they could.

They felt so happy they danced with glee;
But the farmer's wife came in to see
What might this merrymaking be

Of three Glad Mice.

Three Poor Mice,
Three Poor Mice,

Soon changed their tone,
Soon changed their tone.

The farmer's wife said, "What are you at,
And why were you capering round like that?
Just wait a minute: I'll fetch the cat."

Oh, dear! Poor Mice.

Three Scared Mice,
Three Scared Mice,

Ran for their lives,
Ran for their lives.

They jumped out onto the window ledge;
The mention of "cat" set their teeth on edge,
So they hid themselves in the bramble hedge,

These three Scared Mice.

Three Sad Mice,
Three Sad Mice,

What could they do?
What could they do?

The bramble hedge was most unkind:
It scratched their eyes and made them blind,
And soon each mouse went out of his mind,

These three Sad Mice.

Three Blind Mice,
Three Blind Mice,

See how they run!
See how they run!

They all ran after the farmer's wife,
Who cut off their tails with the carving knife.
Did you ever see such a sight in your life

As three Blind Mice?

Three Sick Mice,
Three Sick Mice,

Gave way to tears,
Gave way to tears.

They could not see and they had no end;
They sought a chemist and found a friend.
He gave them some "Never too late to mend,"

These three Sick Mice.

Three Wise Mice,
Three Wise Mice,

Rubbed rubbed away,
Rubbed rubbed away.

And soon their tails began to grow,
And their eyes recovered their sight, you know;
They looked in the glass and it told them so,

These three Wise Mice.

Three Proud Mice,
Three Proud Mice,

Soon settled down,
Soon settled down.

The name of their house I cannot tell,
But they've learned a trade and are doing well.
If you call upon them, ring the bell

Three times twice.

FINIS